JUST PLAIN BOB

Sarah

BECOMING A SHARED WIFE, VOL. 7

HOT EROTICA

WARNING

This book contains sexually explicit scenes and adult language. It may be considered offensive to some readers. This book is for sale to adults ONLY.

* * * * * * * * * * * * * * * * * * *

Please store your files wisely where they cannot be accessed by underage readers.

Please feel free to send me an email. Just know that these emails are filtered by my publisher. Good news is always welcome.

Just Plain Bob - **justplainbob@awesomeauthors.org**

About the Publisher

4Fun Publishing, a member of **BLVNP Incorporated**, 340 S. Lemon #6200, Walnut CA 91789, info@blvnp.com / legal@blvnp.com
NOTE: Due to the highly emotional reaction of some people to works of erotic fiction, any email sent to the above address that contains foul language or religious references is automatically deleted by our anti-spam software and will not be seen. All other communications are welcome.

DISCLAIMER

Sarah

Becoming a Shared Wife, Vol. 7

Hot Erotica

By: Just Plain Bob

© **Just Plain Bob 2014**
ISBN: 978-1-68030-082-6

Chapter 1

Sarah looked down at the sleeping form on the bed and once again wondered what was wrong with her. She loved Tim with all her heart and she knew that she would die for him if need be so how could she do to him what she was doing? It would be one thing if Tim was lousy in bed, but he was a wonderful lover. And it wasn't because they did not get along; they had a wonderful and loving relationship. After having seen the way the marriages of some of her friends were she knew just how blessed she was. So what was it? Was there such a thing as a slut gene? A gene that made you a cock crazy slut? Whatever it was that caused her to do what she was doing she prayed to God that Tim would never find out.

$$\sim\sim***\sim\sim$$

Sarah had been a virgin when she met Tim during their junior year at college. Since early in high school she'd had hundreds of opportunities to rid herself of that condition, but she had been determined to give that prize to the man she married. That hadn't meant that she couldn't be a fun date. If she liked a guy, really liked him, he could get a hand job out of her and if she really, really liked him, a blowjob was not out of the question, but it was going to take love to get 'her pearl of great price.'

She found love at the college bookstore when she and Tim had bumped into each other, literally, causing her to fall to the floor and drop her books. Tim had apologized profusely as he had helped her pick up what she had dropped. When she had looked into his eyes she felt the tingle all the way down to her toes. For her, it had been love at first sight and she knew that she didn't dare let him get away so she had done something that she had never done before – she went after him. Since the day her breasts had just started poking out, while she was still getting used to the training bra, she had been the pursued, but with Tim she became the pursuer. She brazenly told him that his apology would only be accepted if he bought her coffee at the Student Union cafeteria.

Tim never had a chance once she set her sights on him. She had put on a full court press and at the end of their junior year, Tim had asked her to marry him and she had accepted. From her standpoint, their wedding night had been Heavenly and it never changed. At the end of five years of marriage, they were still making love a half dozen times a week. She was blessed and she knew it. She was deeply in love with Tim and he with her and life could not have been more perfect.

~~***~~

It had been the night of Tim's company Christmas party. She loved dressing sexy and letting everybody see just how lucky Tim was and she outdid herself for the party. Little black dress (with no bra), four-inch heels, a single strand of pearls around her neck and hair and makeup done just right. As she looked at herself in the mirror, she was happy with the result. The look was sexy, but elegant and the proof was that Tim kept trying to get her to lift the hem of her dress for a quickie before the party. She was tempted, but she knew that if she held him off, he would be so charged up when they got home that the sex would be mind-blowing.

She made a point to sit close to him on the drive to the party and to rub his cock through his trousers while she told him what she had in store for him later in the evening.

"I'm going to flirt with your co-workers baby. I'm going to tease you and every other man I see tonight. I might even let one or two of them think they might get lucky. I'm going to have you so hot by the time we get home that your dick will stay hard for a week."

And she had. Several men besides Tim danced with her that night and if a cock touched her leg or belly, no matter how accidentally, she leaned into it. A hand dropping to her ass was an invitation for her to push her pelvis forward and a hand straying to her breast caused her to maneuver so her back was to anyone who could see it. One hand went down inside her dress and fingers tweaked one of her nipples and all she did was smile at the man.

"Naughty, naughty boy. You know those don't belong to you," she said.

Every man she danced with got her under the mistletoe and every kiss got some tongue from her. After every dance, she would go back to the table, reach under it and place her hand on Tim's rock hard cock and grin at him.

"Can you hold it baby, or are you going to end up taking me right here on the table in front of God and everybody?"

"Keep it up Sarah and I'll cum in my pants so many times before we get home that I won't be able to get it up for you after we get there."

"Don't you worry about that lover. I'll see to it that I get you up."

The party was three hours old when she got up to go to the bathroom. She did her business, refreshed her makeup and just before she left the bathroom she grinned as she had a wicked thought. She took off her panties and tucked them in her purse. When she got back to the table, she would take Tim's hand and run it up under her dress. She giggled as she thought that maybe, just maybe, she could make him cum in his pants.

She was walking back to the party when a door opened, an arm shot out, grabbed her arm and pulled her into the room. She was spun around, bent over a desk and a hand in the middle of her back held her down. She heard a zipper being pulled down and she smiled.

"Couldn't wait till we got home baby?" she asked as she spread her legs wide. "Come on lover, put it in me. Fuck your slut baby, make me scream."

The cock lanced into her pussy, already sopping wet from her teasing, and she moaned.

"Oh yes lover, oh yes. Hard lover, fuck me hard."

The cock drove into her as hands held her hips and she felt her orgasm coming. "Harder baby, harder. Oh God Timmy, you feel so good, you feel so god damned good."

Her body shook and she gave a long low moan as she came and only seconds later she felt the warmth in her pussy as Tim spent himself.

"Bad boy," she said, as she lifted herself off the desk. "You were supposed to wait until we got home."

She turned and got the shock of her life. It wasn't Tim! She had just been fucked by Tim's boss, Brian Tyler! The two of the stood there staring at each other for several seconds and then, and she never understood why, she bent and took Brian's cock in her mouth and licked and sucked on it until he was hard again. She turned and bent over the desk.

"Again."

She had an orgasm as soon as Brian slid into her and then she had two more as he fucked her that second time and when he came in her she got up from the desk and walked out of the room. The only word spoken between them, from start to finish, had been when she had said, "Again."

She had gone back to the bathroom and had cleaned herself out as best she could and then she had rejoined Tim at the table. Once seated, she had taken his hand up under her dress as she spread her legs.

"See how wet I am for you, lover? Would you like to get under the table and lick my wet pussy?" She giggled and reached over to touch the hard lump in Tim's pants. "Pants aren't wet yet, lover. I guess I'll have to try harder."

The next hour and a half was more of the same – drinking, dancing and teasing. Then Tim looked at his watch and told her that it was time to leave.

"I'll need to hit the john first baby, I don't think I'll be able to hold it until we get home."

She looked around the room and found Brian and her eyes held his for several seconds and then she got up and headed for the bathrooms. She was sitting on the desk when Brian came into the room and as soon as he entered, she laid back, spread her legs and waited. He entered her and her legs had gone up and wrapped around him and she pushed her hips up to meet his and then she started having what felt like a continuous orgasm as Brian fucked her to orgasm after orgasm. In five years of what had been a very active sex life with Tim, she had never cum so many times in so short a period. When Brian came in her for the third time that night, she had orgasmed once more and it had been so intense that she had screamed. When he pulled out of her she had stood up, straightened her dress, said, "Call me," and had walked out of the room.

She and Tim were no sooner in the car than she was next to him and pulling down his zipper. She bent her head, took him in her mouth and within seconds he had bathed the back of her throat with his juices. She took her mouth off him long enough to say, "I'm glad we got the quick one out of the way," and she went back to sucking on him. As soon as she was in the front door she kicked off her heels and headed for the bedroom pulling her dress over her head on the way. She had the covers down and was lying on the bed with her legs spread and ready for him when he came into the room. By the time he reached the bed, he was naked and he climbed on the bed.

"I don't usually do this until we get the first fuck out of the way, but you have got to be steaming hot and I just have to have a taste."

He lowered his head toward her pussy and she panicked and was about to shout, "No, you can't," when she realized he would ask why. She knew she couldn't say, "Because I still have Brian's cum in me," and she didn't have time enough to come up with any good reason. Tim's tongue slipped between her pussy lips and for the second time that night she had an orgasm at the instant she was entered. As she settled down, she bit her lip and waited to see if Tim would notice the salty taste of what he was licking up and comment on it.

He stopped licking her and looked up at her and she braced herself for the worst, but all Tim said was "I don't believe you have ever been this wet before. I think your teasing did as big a number on you as it did on the guys you teased."

She breathed a sigh of relief as her husband went back to licking up the juices left in her by his boss. The sheer wickedness of it gave her another orgasm before Tim moved up and unknowingly took the first sloppy seconds he had ever gotten from his wife.

She made love with Tim twice more that night before he went to sleep. She snuggled up next to him and thought back on the night's events. Why had she not slapped Brian's face, kicked him in the balls and run to Tim to tell him what had happened? Why had she sucked Brian's cock and then asked him to do her again? And the third time, she had as much as invited him to follow her and why in God's name had she told him to call her? She fell asleep with none of those questions answered.

~~***~~

It was three days later when Brian called her at work. All he said when he got her on the phone was, "Care to have a long lunch with me?"

She hadn't even hesitated. "How long?"

"As long as you can make it."

"Where?"

"The Hampton House, room 312 and as soon as you can get there."

"If I leave now I can be there in fifteen minutes."

"I'll be waiting."

"Now why did I do that?" She asked herself as she put down the phone. "All I had to do was say no or hang up and that would have been the end of it. Then again, maybe not. I did tell him to call and he might keep trying. Better I go meet him and tell him face to face why the night of the party was a mistake and that it can never happen again."

Brian had answered her knock already stripped down to his boxers, which were already tented. She stared at the bulge and the little speech she had prepared was forgotten as she walked into the room and started removing her clothes. Brian moved to the bed, removed his boxers and lay down on his back with his erect cock pointing up at the ceiling.

"Leave the heels on," he said as she removed her panties. She moved to the bed and still not having said a word to him, she lowered her head and took his cock in her mouth. She licked and sucked him until he announced that he was going to cum and then she pushed her mouth down on him and deep throated him as he bathed the back of her throat with his cum. She swallowed every drop, sucked the last couple out of his pee hole and then went back to licking and sucking on him until he was hard again.

Once hard, she moved up and swung over him. Using her right hand to guide him into her she lowered herself down on his erection until their pubic hairs intertwined and then she began to ride him. After several minutes of her pounding down on him, Brian gripped her and rolled her over onto her back and began fucking her hard. Sharp little cries and low moans were the only sounds from her as Brian pounded himself into her pussy. She felt her orgasm coming and she hissed out a, "Yeeessssss, oooh yeeesssss," as it hit and she shoved her pussy up at Brian, grabbed the cheeks of his ass and pulled him tight to her.

"Yesssss," she hissed and then, "Oh God, oh God, Oh God," followed by a scream as her body was shaken by a massive orgasm. Her nails bit into Brian's ass as she tried to pull him deep inside her and then she felt his hot cum splash the inner walls of her pussy. Brian held himself in her until his cock was soft and then he pulled out of her and said, "I want your tight little ass next," and then he lay down on the bed beside her.

She got up on her knees, moved over until her head was over his cock and then she lowered it, captured his cock and went to work on getting him hard again. It took her several minutes, but he began to harden and when he was hard enough she moved up to the head of the bed, lowered her head onto a pillow and waited. Brian took his time and used his fingers and thumb to work her butt hole and loosen it up and then he slid his cock into her sperm filled pussy to get some lube on his dick. He stroked into her several times and then he pulled out of her pussy and put the head of his cock against her anal rosebud and then gently started to work it into her.

She spoke her first words since coming into the room:

"Careful lover, it's my first time. Tim won't do me there. Go easy lover, go easy on me."

She felt some pain and discomfort, but no more than she had felt when she had given up her virginity. The pain and discomfort slowly gave way to a somewhat pleasurable feeling and in another minute she was pushing her ass back to meet Brian's strokes. Brian noticed that she was getting into it and he started fucking her just a little harder and faster. She was surprised when she felt the tingle that told her an orgasm was starting to build deep inside her. How could that be? Anal sex couldn't give you an orgasm, could it? There was no denying the feeling; she'd had it way too often not to recognize it. Could it be simply because she was cheating on Tim with his boss? The wickedness of forbidden sex? The erotic thought that she was going to go home to her husband full of another man's cum? Whatever the reason her body suddenly craved the cock in her ass. She moaned and pushed herself back at Brian.

"Oh yes, yes, yes," she moaned, "Push it in. Go deeper, fuck my ass, fuck my ass, fuck it hard."

Brian started ramming his cock into her shit hole and she cried, moaned and begged him to fuck her harder.

"I'm doing the best I can," Brian gasped as he continued pounding into her.

"Oh God, oh God, oh God," she moaned over and over as she pushed her ass back at him. She could feel the orgasm hovering just out of reach and she desperately wanted it. "Fuck me damn you, fuck me. Fuck me hard, make me cum."

Brian put on a quick burst of speed, slamming into her butt hole as hard as he could and suddenly she screamed out, "OH YES, OH GOD YES!!!!" as the orgasm took hold of her. She relaxed her body as Brian continued to pound into her and with her head buried in the pillow she felt the first stirrings of shame. Not because she was cheating on Tim with his boss, but because she had let a man other than her husband give her her first anal orgasm. Brian was still thrusting into her hard and she started shoving her ass back at him to try and help him get off. She really did need to get back to work and maybe she could spend some time sitting at her desk, staring out the window and trying to figure out how this had started and why she was allowing it to continue. After another minute or so Brian groaned, "Here it comes, here it comes, oh god, so fucking good," as he shot his sperm into her butt hole.

As she was dressing Brian said, "I've reserved this room for the same time every Tuesday for the next month."

She had looked at him for several seconds and then she had nodded a yes. She finished dressing and left the room. In the elevator, she again asked herself why she was letting this happen and again she didn't have an answer. As she exited the elevator in the lobby, she realized that she had never really talked with Brian. Outside of the moaning, pleading and exhortations during the sexual act, she had not said a word to him other than the "again," and the "call me" of the first time and the please go easy on her ass of this time. She had never even kissed him.

"What the hell is wrong with me?" she asked herself as she headed back to her office. "I have the greatest husband in the world and I love him to death and yet I just agreed to meet a man I don't even know well enough to know whether or not I even like him for sex every Tuesday for the next month."

What was it that she didn't know about herself? What was it that Brian saw when he looked at her? He had known she wouldn't cry rape when he did what he did. He somehow looked at her and knew she would be his willing slut. How could he have possibly known she wouldn't run straight to Tim and tell him what happened. How could he have been so sure that she wouldn't call the police? Well, she hadn't done any of those things had she? All she had done was spread her legs wide and open her mouth for him. And it seemed that she was going to continue doing it.

Chapter 2

For the next three weeks the pattern was the same. She would meet Brian in room 312 of the Hampton and Brian would answer the door already stripped down to his boxers. She would strip, put her high heels back on and then climb on the bed and suck him off. She would keep sucking until he was hard again and then he would fuck her to several orgasms and after he came she would suck him hard again and then he would take her ass. They never kissed and she never did more than nod her head when he told her something. He never asked, he just told her what he wanted and she always nodded a yes.

The fourth Tuesday, she broke the pattern. After taking Brian in her ass she got up and washed his cock off and then deep throated him to get him up again and then she took him in her pussy for the second time that day. She also spoke to him for the first time.

"I don't have to go back to work today so don't be surprised if you aren't able to walk out of this room when I'm done with you."

"My God, she does have a voice. Does this mean I should take the room for another month?"

"Just shut up and fuck me."

"Well just so you know, I'm taking the room for next Tuesday, but the next two Tuesdays after that I'm going to fuck you on your own bed."

She looked up at him startled. "Why are you doing this to me? Why are you trying to ruin my marriage?"

"I'm not trying to ruin your marriage, I'm just taking advantage of a situation."

"I don't understand; what situation?"

I'm sending Tim to Seattle next week to negotiate the Byrnes contract and the following week he will be in San Diego to work with Sullivan. He is the best man for the job and he would be going even if you weren't fucking me. He will be gone, your bed will be empty and I'm going to keep his side of it warm for him."

She stared at him not knowing what to say. He smiled at her, "You still haven't figured it out have you?"

"Figured out what?"

"Why you are letting me stuff my cock in your mouth, cunt and ass."

Again she had no idea what to say.

"Well I'll tell you. You are my slut because you wanted to be someone's slut and I was the first to recognize it and do something about it."

She started to tell him he was wrong, but he held up a hand and said:

"Hear me out first. Let me say up front that Tim has never talked to me about you so what I am going to say are things that I know. Things that I know from watching you. I just know. I can't even begin to tell you how I know, I just do. You were a virgin when you got married. You were sexually active to the extent that you gave a lot of hand jobs and probably a good two dozen blowjobs. You probably don't even realize that in the back of your mind you have always been curious about what being fucked by a cock other than Tim's would be like. It was obvious to me at the Christmas party, from the way you were dressed and the way you acted that you were offering yourself to anyone who had the balls to take you. I had the stones to do it and here we are."

"You are crazy if you think that."

"Deny it all you want Sarah, but you are here. Pretend I'm crazy all you want, but I have been fucking you for over a month now and you have made no attempt to stop me. The night of the party it was you who wanted the second and third time. I'll tell you something else that you don't know. I'm the first, but I won't be the last. There are at least four or five more cocks in your future before you settle down and go back to being a one man woman for Tim."

She was shaken by his certainty. He was wrong; he had to be wrong. Five more? No way!

"You don't know what you are talking about. Now, are you going to fuck me or should I get dressed and leave?"

"Not to worry Sarah, I'm going to fuck you and I'm going to keep on fucking you until you decide to stop."

~~***~~

That evening she almost experienced firsthand how a cheating wife can plant suspicion in the mind of her husband. She and Tim were at the dinner table and were talking about their respective days at work and having general conversation and she had a sudden thought.

"Do you have any idea where our suitcases are?"

"No, but I expect that they are down in the basement someplace. Why?"

"Because you…" and she caught herself just in time. She had been about to say that he would need them for his trip, but he hadn't told her about the trip yet and she didn't even know if Brian had mentioned the trip to Tim.

"Because why Sarah?"

Thinking quickly she said, "I talked to my mom this morning and she said dad is having some health problems. I may need to go visit."

"Nothing serious I hope."

"I don't know, she wouldn't give me the details."

The lie wasn't even all the way out of her mouth before she realized she had screwed up again. What if her mother did call and Tim answered the phone and asked about how her father was coming along. Her mother would say, "Fine, why do you ask?" Tim would say, "Sarah said when she talked to you last Tuesday that he was having health problems," and her mother would say, "Last Tuesday? I haven't talked with Sarah in almost three weeks."

One tiny lie to cover a slip over the suitcases and then a bigger lie to cover the first one and then on and on and on. She was going to have to be careful, super careful, about what she did and what she said. It would kill her if Tim found out what she was doing. He would be gone in a heartbeat and she knew that she couldn't bear living without him. Right then and there she resolved that whatever it was she had going with Brian was over and done with. Whatever it was that they had going was not worth losing Tim over.

Every day for the rest of the week she smothered Tim with love and affection and she had put Brian completely out of her mind, but on Friday he was back. Over dinner Tim asked:

"Did you ever find those suitcases?"

"I never looked for them. Why?"

"The company is sending me out of town to negotiate some contracts."

"When?"

"Week after next."

"How long will you be gone?"

"For two weeks."

"You had better stock up on vitamins then."

"Why?"

"If I'm only going to have you for the rest of this week and next week I probably won't let you leave the bedroom."

"Maybe we should skip dessert and go to bed now so you can stock up – build up some reserves – to hold you until I get back."

"I like the way you think lover. The dishes can wait, let's go."

~~***~~

Tuesday noon found her outside the door to room 312. The easy way to do it would have been to simply not show up, but she had convinced herself that doing it that way would leave the door open for Brian to call her and keep calling her. No, the way to do it was face to face. Impress on Brian that it was over and that they would never see each other again. She took a deep breath, steeled her resolve and then knocked on the door.

Brian answered the door in his boxers as usual and he moved aside to let her in. She walked into the room and then froze as Brian closed the door behind her. There on the bed in front of her, naked and with an erection pointing straight up at the ceiling, was her boss. Brian moved up behind her, reached around and cupped her breasts in his hands as he said:

"You know Dave. Dave and I went to school together and we belonged to the same fraternity. We met for dinner and drinks last Saturday and imagine my surprise at finding out you work for him. Imagine his surprise when he found out that you are my slut and that I have been fucking you for over a month now. I can just imagine your surprise at finding out that fraternity brothers share their sluts. You will no doubt be pleased to know that Dave isn't expecting you to return to work this afternoon. I think you should thank him for that, don't you?"

Her eyes were locked on Dave's cock as she undid the buttons on her blouse. It was longer and a little fatter than Brian's and it had a slight curve to the left. As she kicked her skirt away, she wondered how it was going to feel and five minutes later she had the answer to that question – it felt marvelous.

It was a long afternoon for her and an afternoon full of firsts. It was her first time with two men. It was the first time she had ever been on her knees in front of two sitting men while she alternated sucking their cocks. It was the first time she'd had a cock in her mouth and pussy at the same time, the first time she'd had a cock in her mouth an ass at the same time and the first time she had experienced a cock in her ass and pussy at the same time. And it was her first gangbang, or was it? Were two men a gangbang? Well two men were definitely a gang as far as she was concerned.

She thought back to the previous Tuesday and what Brian had said about there being more cocks in her future and now she thought that just maybe he knew what he was talking about. She was already wondering what it would be like to have a third cock that she could take in her mouth while she had one in her pussy and one in her ass. Did Dave and Brian have another frat brother available? Did she dare ask? Her train of thought was broken as Dave pulled out of her ass and lay down on the bed.

"Come on Sarah, make me hard again."

"Not until you go and wash that filthy thing."

"You're a slut Sarah and sluts suck dirty cocks."

"I'll grant you that I have done some pretty slutty things here this afternoon, but I'm not doing that. Now go wash it or the only place it is going to go is back in my ass."

"You're no fun Sarah," he said as he rolled off the bed and headed for the bathroom.

~~***~~

It was four-thirty when she pushed Dave away as he was going for her butt again.

"Sorry, but I need to clean up and get home to fix dinner for my hubby."

As she was leaving, Dave asked her when he could see her again and she said she would see him at work the next day.

"That's not what I meant Sarah. When can we do this again?"

"I don't think we can. I came here today to tell Brian that it was over."

"Then why didn't you turn and leave when you saw me here?"

"I don't know. I really don't know."

"Of course you know Sarah," Brian said, "Four or five I said, remember? Now it is only three or four more."

"I told you that you were wrong about that. There won't be any more. I don't even know why I've done this much."

"You might not know Sarah, but I do," Dave said. "You are a natural born slut. It has been lying dormant in you and somehow Brian recognized it and brought it out in the open."

"No, you are wrong. I am not a slut! I have to go."

As she reached for the doorknob, Brian said that he would walk her out and he followed her out the door and down the hall to the elevator.

In the elevator Brian said, "Did you mean it when you said that you came here today to end it?"

"Yes, I did."

"Give me two more weeks and I promise you I'll never bother you again. I won't call you and I won't try and see you."

"Why two more weeks?"

"I want you the two weeks that Tim is going to be gone. After that I'm out of your life."

"I don't know Brian, I really need to put a stop to things before something happens and Tim finds out."

"Two weeks Sarah, that's all I'm asking. If anything, you owe me that much for today."

"Why do I owe you for today?"

"Because you had the time of your life this afternoon. You loved every second of it and I'd bet good money that at one point during the afternoon you were wishing that a third cock had been available for you to play with."

How could he know that? She wondered and was surprised when he laughed.

"Bingo," he said, "Your expression tells me that I hit the nail right on the head. Come on, Sarah, two weeks, just give me two weeks. Look at it this way. Tim is gone, you love cock so if you don't give me the two weeks, you will have to go without it for two weeks. You don't want that, do you? Think about it, Sarah. I'll give you a call on Monday when Tim is on his flight."

Chapter 3

On the way home Sarah wondered what kind of excuse she could use if Tim wanted to make love that night. A good douche would take care of the sloppy wetness, but she couldn't think of anything that would tighten her pussy up other than time. She would have to stall Tim at least for a day and maybe even two. One more reason to put a stop to what she was doing. It just wasn't right that Tim should be denied his rights as a husband because she couldn't seem to say no to Brian. Well she was going to say no. She was not going to give him the two weeks that Tim was gone. Brian had seen the last of her.

However, she did have a fresh problem to work out – Dave! From the way he had acted he was obviously expecting to have more sex with her and she would need to shut him down, but she would have to do it in a nice way. If she had to she could tell Brian to go piss up a rope, but she couldn't do that with Dave, not and expect to continue working for him. She would be polite, but firm. She would tell him that it had been enjoyable, but that it was a one-time thing. She would tell him that she loved her husband and valued her marriage and that she could never again do anything that would put it at risk. Dave was married so he should understand where she was coming from. Yes, that was the way to do it, polite but firm.

~~***~~

She had been at work almost an hour when Jenny, Dave's secretary (and also his daughter), called her and told her that Dave wanted to see her in his office. She thought nothing of it as she usually got called to his office a couple of times a day to give progress reports. When she got to Dave's office, Jenny told her to go right in.

Dave was sitting behind his desk and he smiled when he saw her.

"Get a good night's sleep?" he asked

"Yes, why?"

"Oh nothing, I just wondered. I always sleep great after I've exercised and I sure got some great exercise yesterday afternoon."

She had blushed at that. "Yes, well I need to talk with you about that, Dave. It was a great afternoon and I really…" And Dave held up a hand to cut her off.

"Not know Sarah. Right now I have something for you to do that needs to be taken care of immediately."

"Of course Dave, what is it?"

Dave pushed back from his desk and she saw that his cock was out of his fly and it was erect and throbbing. "I need you to take care of this," and he got up and walked around the desk toward her.

Her eyes were on his hard cock as it bobbed up and down as he walked to her and she tore them away and said, "Actually Dave, I was about to tell you tha…" and Dave moved behind her and bent her forward over his desk.

"Lift your skirt and spread your legs Sarah."

"But Dave, I don…"

"Just do it Sarah. Lift your skirt and spread your legs, now."

Her voice quivered as she said, "Yes Dave," and did what he'd told her. She felt his fingers push the gusset of her panties aside and then the head of his cock touched her pussy and she moaned as he pushed in.

"Oh yes Sarah, you like that don't you? You like starting the day out like this and that is a good thing because this is how we will start every day from now on. A blowjob or a fuck, or maybe even both. You understand Sarah?"

She spread her legs a bit wider and pushed back at him and moaned, "Yes Dave."

~~***~~

On the drive home that night she was on the verge of tears the whole way. Why did she let Brian and Dave do what they were doing to her? Why did she do it to Tim? She loved him; he was her entire world so why was she letting Brian and Dave take her body when they wanted it? It wasn't because they were exceptional in bed; Tim was much better than either of them and it certainly had nothing to do with cock size because Tim had them beat there also. She had to stop what she was doing before Tim found out. She couldn't lose him, she just couldn't.

The next morning when Jenny called and said that Dave wanted to see her in his office, she walked in determined to put an end to their sexual liaisons.

"Dave, we have to talk."

"All right Sarah, but first you need to come over here and take care of this."

He rolled his chair back from his desk and just as the previous day his erection was sticking up out of his fly. "Come over here Sarah, and suck my cock."

"Look Dave, this has got to…"

"Not now Sarah, suck first, talk later."

"No Dave, I don…."

"God damn it Sarah, stop fucking around and get over here."

She stood there staring at his throbbing cock, watching it twitch and her knees felt weak and then almost inaudibly she said, "Yes Dave, whatever you want."

She turned and went to the door to lock it but Dave said, "Don't bother. Jenny knows what is going on in here and she won't let anyone in until we are through."

"Jenny knows?"

"Yes Sarah, Jenny knows, now get over here."

"Your daughter knows?"

"Sarah, get over here and suck my cock or get out."

She took one last look at the door and then went over and went to her knees in front of her boss. For some weird reason, the thought that Dave's daughter was sitting right outside the door knowing that she was having sex with Dave made her pussy tingle and she could feel herself getting wet as she lowered her head and engulfed Dave's cock.

And that was just the start of her Thursday. At lunchtime Dave took her on his desk while she grunted and moaned and dug her nails into his back. At four-thirty she was bent forward over his desk as Dave stuffed his cock into her tight ass. She was breathing hard and hissing out a, "Yes, yes, yes, yes," when the door opened and Jenny came in. She stood there watching for a minute or so and then said:

"She certainly seems to enjoy it."

"She's hot and tight," Dave said, "And she loves cock up her ass."

"Melvin likes ass fucking. I won't let him do mine, but maybe you might let him do her."

"Maybe, but not for a while. I'm keeping this for myself."

"Well okay. I just came in to tell you I'm leaving. Good night dad," and then she bent down and looked into Sarah's face. "Good night, Mrs. Clayton" with heavy emphasis on the "Mrs."

"Since you are leaving, lock the door on your way out."

Jenny laughed and said, "What's the matter pops? Afraid someone will come in and you'll have to share?" She laughed again and left the office.

Throughout the exchange she had been breathing hard and shoving her ass back at Dave and reaching out for the orgasm that seemed to be just beyond her reach. As soon as the door clicked behind her she felt her climax hit and she screamed out.

"Like this, do you? I'm going to see to it that you get a lot of it from now on. You are my in house slut from now on Sarah, you understand?"

"Yes Dave."

"Say it Sarah, let me hear you say it."

"I'm your slut Dave."

"And I can have your ass whenever and wherever I want?"

"Yes Dave, whenever and wherever."

Dave picked up her panties, wiped his cock with them and handed them to her. "I ordered a leather couch for the office. It will be delivered sometime tomorrow morning and I'm sure that it will be easier on you than that hard desk."

She stuffed her panties in her purse and said, "Aren't you afraid that Jenny will tell your wife about this?"

"No, Jenny and I have an agreement. She won't tell Mary about what I do and I won't tell Mary that Jenny is fucking our chauffeur."

"Jenny is fucking a nig…black man?"

"Has been for over a year now. You started to say nigger and that's my leverage. Mary was born and raised in the Deep South. If it was some white guy Jenny was screwing, Mary wouldn't give it a second thought. She would just shrug it off as none of her business since Jenny is a grown up now. But a black man? If Mary found out that Jenny likes black meat Mary would disown her."

"Surely Jenny isn't in love with him, is she?"

"I don't know, but why would you ask that?"

"She suggested that you let Melvin do me in my ass."

"What's that got to do with anything?"

"Well, why would she want the man she loves to fuck me?"

"You would have to ask her that."

~~***~~

The couch was delivered Friday at nine and at nine-ten Jenny called her and told her that Dave wanted to see her in his office. When she got there Jenny smiled at her sweetly and said, "Go right on in Mrs. Clayton, he is expecting you." Again she put heavy emphasis on the Mrs. and she wondered why Jenny had stopped calling her Sarah. She didn't have time to spend on that thought though as Dave kept her busy until lunchtime. He greeted her with:

"I hope your desk and calendar are clear because we need to initiate this couch."

Dave sat on it, unzipped his fly and took out his hardening cock. She stood and looked at it as it slowly came erect and she wondered why she didn't just turn and run from the room. So what if Dave fired her, it was only a job and she could get another one. That is what she should do, she thought as she stared at Dave's throbbing cock, just turn and walk out. Her thoughts were interrupted:

"Come on Sarah, time for my slut to start our morning out right."

She stared at his cock and noticed the drop of pre-cum forming in the pee hole and her pussy tingled. "Yes Dave" she said as she sank to her knees in front of him. She lowered her head and took his cock in her mouth.

After she had sucked him to completion and swallowed his juices she kept him in her mouth until he was hard again and then Dave stood her up, bent her over the arm of the couch and fucked her pussy from behind. Another suck session got him hard enough to bend her over the back of the couch and fuck her tight ass, the toes of her high heels barely touching the floor as he pounded into her. He fucked her lying on the couch with her legs up on his shoulders and he fucked her ass a second time while she was on her hands and knees.

After each fuck she had sucked his cock to get it hard again and once, while she was on her hands and knees with Dave's cock in her ass Jenny had come in and placed some papers on her father's desk. She stood and watched her as her dad pounded into Sarah's butt hole and then she said:

"Dad, you just have to let Melvin have a taste of that ass" and then she left.

At noon Dave told her to take the rest of the day off. "I know your husband is leaving for two weeks so go on home and fuck his brains out. Drain him so dry that he won't even think of getting some strange pussy while he is gone."

As she drove home she thought of what Dave had said. She smiled to herself; Tim would never stray, he loved her and he would never do that to her.

~~***~~

When Tim carried his suitcase and briefcase out to the car Monday morning he did look just a bit under the weather. She had taken Dave's advice and had done her level best to fuck Tim's brains out, not to keep him from looking for strange pussy, but because she loved him and was going to miss him. It would be the longest they would be apart since before their wedding.

Her day was a busy one. Her morning call from Dave came at nine and she wasn't surprised that she had been looking forward to it. As much as she agonized over what she was doing behind Tim's back she did have to admit that fucking Dave at work felt deliciously wicked and extremely sexually exciting. After a long and leisurely blowjob she got back to work. She managed to clear her IN basket by the time Dave called her for their 'nooner' on the leather couch. She dealt with client phone calls till four and her pussy was already moist with anticipation when Jenny called her at four-fifteen and told her that Dave wanted her in his office.

As she approached Dave's office she noticed the tall, slim black man standing by Jenny's desk. She nodded to Melvin as she went by him and she noticed his appraising glance. Did he know what she was about to do? The answer to that was probably yes. If he was Jenny's lover she probably had told him. She wondered if Jenny had told him about how much she liked getting anal sex from Dave.

When she entered the office Dave was ready for what she had expected. His cock was hard and sticking out his fly and he greeted her with a smile and told her to lean over the back of the couch.

"I want your ass this time."

She smiled as she took off her panties because that is what she wanted too. She tossed her panties on Dave's desk and leaned over the back of the couch.

"Hurry Dave, I've been wanting this all day."

"Not to worry you sweet little slut, I'll see to it that you don't miss Tim's cock while he is gone."

He eased into her back passage and she moaned as inch by inch she took him in. She was momentarily ashamed that she had never had Tim in her ass. He always said that the very idea was disgusting and he would never try her butt even when she had asked him to. Then she lost that thought as the pleasure of Dave's fucking took over.

Leaning over the back of the couch with just the toes of her 'come fuck me' heels touching the floor she had no leverage to push back at Dave; all she could do was beg him to fuck her hard and make her cum. She was moaning and grunting out.

"Oh yes baby, oh yes, so good, so fucking good!" when the office door opened and Jenny came in carrying a cordless phone. Behind Jenny she saw Melvin standing in the door watching her take Dave's cock up her ass and she remembered that Jenny had said that Melvin loved butt fucking, but that she wouldn't let him do it to her. She wondered what Melvin was thinking as he watched Dave drive into her butt hole. He probably wants some she thought and then she wondered what a black cock would be like. She wondered if it was true what she'd heard about blacks. Her thoughts were interrupted by Jenny handing her the phone.

"It's for you Mrs. Clayton. I hated to interrupt, but he says it is important."

She took the phone and it was Brian. "I just wanted to confirm that we are on for tonight."

Just then Dave drove into her hard and she cried out, "Yes, oh yes," and Brian chuckled and said, "Eager huh? I like that in a woman. See you tonight at six," and he disconnected.

"Oh shit," she thought, "I wasn't going to have any more to do with him. I'll just tell him goodbye when he comes to the door; I won't even let him come in off the porch."

Dave had kept pounding her while she was on the phone and he had gotten her right to the edge of an orgasm and she dropped the phone, grabbed a cushion and she screamed out.

"Oh yes, oh yes, oh God yes, yes, yes!" as she came.

Jenny was still standing there and Melvin was still watching from the doorway when Jenny said, "You just have to give Melvin a shot at that ass pops."

"No way Jenny, Melvin is yours to take care of. This one is mine for now. I might share later, but not now."

"Spoil sport," Jenny said as she turned and left the room.

Chapter 4

Sarah got home at twenty after five and began working on the speech she was going to give Brian. She would tell him that she loved Tim deeply and didn't want to lose him, which is what was sure to happen if she got caught cheating on him.

"And I would get caught," she would say. "Sooner or later I'd make a slip or do something that would make him suspicious. The only way to keep that from happening is to stop things right now."

Brain would be upset, but she would soften the blow by stroking his ego. She would say something like, "I'm glad it happened and I enjoyed it very much and if it wasn't for Tim I'd climb in your bed in a heartbeat." She would be nice, she would let him down gently, but she would definitely end it.

Brain rang the doorbell at five to six and as she went to answer it she told herself, "Be firm, be nice about it, but be firm."

When the bedside phone rang at eight o'clock she took her mouth off Brian's cock and rolled over to answer it. Brian grabbed her arm and said to let it ring.

"I can't. It is probably Tim and he expects me to be here."

As she reached for the phone Brian grabbed her and spun her around and drove his cock into her pussy just as she picked up the phone and said hello.

"Hi baby, how are you?"

"Nothing much, just sitting here watching television and wishing you were here."

Brian was now fucking her with slow strokes and she was trying hard not to start pushing her ass back at him. If she stayed completely still she might be able to hold off the orgasm that she knew would be coming.

"How was your day, get much accomplished?"

"That's good isn't it?"

Brian was fucking her a little harder and faster now and he had reached under her and was squeezing her breasts. She was doing her best to try and stay calm and keep from making any noise that might make Tim suspicious. But he picked up on something.

"No baby, just a little edgy. I'm used to you making love to me five or six times a week and I'm sitting here knowing I'm not going to see you for two weeks."

Just then Brain slammed into her hard and she almost lost it. She started to pull away from Brian and he gripped her hips firmly to keep her impaled on his cock. She smacked his right hand hard with the phone receiver and he pulled his hands back and she pulled herself off him.

"What's that baby?"

"I dropped the phone."

"No, I was going to sneeze and I grabbed for the Kleenex and you know how uncoordinated I can be at times."

"No, nothing really, except to say that I love you and I miss you and I need you."

"Okay baby, I'll talk to you tomorrow."

"Love you too, bye."

She hung up the phone and looked back over her shoulder at Brian. He was grinning at her and she giggled and said, "You're so bad."

"I know Sarah and I also know that you love it."

"I guess I do, don't I. I'm off the phone now; you don't have to go easy anymore. Fuck me hard lover, make me cum."

~~***~~

When Brian woke up in the morning she already had her mouth wrapped around his cock and when he was fully awake and fully erect she swung over him and lowered herself down on his hardness. She rode him until he was on the verge of cumming and then she rolled over onto her back and whispered.

"Start my day out right lover. Fuck me hard," and Brian began slamming his cock in her. In just minutes she felt him explode inside her and she pushed him off her, licked his cock clean and headed for the shower. She hadn't gotten off, but it didn't bother her because she knew that Dave would get her off several times before the day was over.

The rest of that week was more of the same. Brian came over and spent the night, fucking her while she was talking with Tim and then waking up in her bed in the morning. At work, Dave was doing her three times a day. The week flew by and as the weekend approached she was looking forward to a little rest and relaxation, but it was not to be.

As had happened all week, Brian had stayed the night Friday and she was busy sliding up and down on his cock on Saturday morning when the doorbell rang. She disengaged herself from Brian, put on a robe and went to the door. She knew who it was before she reached the door because through the living room window she could see Dave's limo parked out front.

"Good morning," Dave said when she opened the door. "I just happened to be in the neighborhood and I thought I'd stop by for a blowjob and then maybe a day of wild sex."

She looked at him for several seconds and then she stepped aside and let him in. Dave waved at Melvin and the limo drove off. When she led Dave into the bedroom, he didn't seem all that surprised to find a naked Brian lying on the bed. Without a word to Dave she got back on the bed and lowered herself down on Brian's pole and went back to riding it. Out of the corner of her eye she saw Dave getting undressed and when he climbed up on the bed and moved behind her she knew what he wanted to do and she shivered in anticipation because she wanted it too. She leaned forward to lie on Brian's chest and that elevated her ass just right for Dave. She groaned as he began working his cock into her butt hole. He and Brian started fucking her and they soon got into a rhythm and she abandoned herself to them.

The two men took turns on her most of the morning and early afternoon. Around three Dave used the bedside phone to make dinner reservations at Anton's and the two men carried her into the shower where they played some more. The limo was waiting when they left the house and Melvin drove them to the restaurant. She saw Melvin looking at her in the mirror and she wondered what he was thinking. When they got to Anton's Dave told Melvin to be back for them by seven-thirty in order to get her home in time for Tim's nightly phone call.

She had Brian's cock in her mouth and was sliding up and down on Dave's cock when the phone rang at eight-ten.

"Sorry baby," she said to Brian, but you are just in the wrong hole for this" and she picked up the phone.

"Hello?"

"Hi lover, miss me?"

"Yeah? Well I'm sure missing you," she said as Dave slowly worked himself up and down in her pussy. She reached out and took hold of Brian's cock and tugged at him to get it next to her mouth.

"This is the longest we have ever been apart baby and I'm not used to going this long without your loving."

She licked the head of Brian's cock and then sucked it into her mouth while she listened to what Tim was saying. When he finished she took her mouth off Brian's cock.

"I've got my finger in my pussy right now lover. I'm imagining that it is your cock filling me up."

Dave thrust up into her and she moaned.

"What's that baby? Oh, that was just me rubbing my clit."

She was slowly working up and down on Dave's cock while stroking Brian and occasionally licking his cock head.

"Oh Jesus baby, I'm so damned horny I could scream." I a voice husky with emotion she said, "Take your cock out for me baby. Do you have it in your hand? Good. Stroke it for me baby. Think of my hot, wet mouth on it. Close your eyes baby; close them and imagine your cock in my mouth. Listen to the sounds I make as I lick and suck my thumb while I pretend it is your cock."

She pulled Brian's cock into her mouth and then held the phone's mouthpiece close to her mouth as Dave fucked her and she sucked Brian's cock. Small moans, grunts and slurping sounds flew through the phone lines from her to Tim. The slutishness of it wound her up and she felt a small orgasm coming.

She pulled her mouth off of Brian and moaned, "This one is for you baby. It is the best my fingers can do, but it is for you," and then

Tim got to listen to her orgasm as Brian jacked off his cock and shot his cum all over her face. An instant later Dave shot his load into her cunt.

"Oh God baby, that was not a good move on my part. I got myself off, but now I'm hornier than ever. Hurry home baby, I need you."

"All right baby, I'll talk to you tomorrow."

"I love you too baby, bye."

She hung up the phone, "One of you guys better hurry up and get hard. I need to be fucked and fucked hard. I don't care how you do it, suck each other if you have to, but I'm going to the bathroom and I want a hard cock when I come back."

They were both up when she got back, not as hard as she would have liked, but stiff enough for penetration and in seconds she had Brian in her ass and Dave in her pussy and she was screaming as they both pounded away.

The two men used her (or she used them) for another hour and then Dave called Melvin to come and pick him up. "Much as I'd like to stay and play I do have a wife I have to get home too. Luckily she spent all day visiting her sick grandmother so I was able to stop by."

She had looked at his still hard cock and asked how much time they had before Melvin got there.

"Maybe an hour. Time enough for you to help me get rid of this," and he waved his hard dick at her and she smiled and went after it.

Brian and Dave had cum so many times that day that by that point they were extremely long lasting and they were constantly bringing her to orgasm. The two men were fucking her so hard that she was in a constant state of arousal and she really wasn't aware of much of what was going on around her. It came as a complete surprise when she noticed Jenny lying next to her on the king-sized bed with Melvin between her legs and fucking her hard. She had no recollection of Jenny even coming into the room, let alone getting on the bed with her. She glanced at Dave and he didn't seem to care that his daughter was lying next to him and being fucked by his black chauffeur.

Dave finally came and announced that he was going to take a shower before dressing and going home to his wife. Jenny got up to go to the bathroom and as soon as she was out of the room Melvin scooted over to her and offered his black cock to her mouth. She looked at it, black and glistening with Jenny's juices, and saw that it was bigger than Dave's and Brian's, but not Tim's. It was not the huge cock that she had expected a black man to have. She leaned forward and her lips closed around Melvin's black hardness just as Dave came back into the room.

"Not now Melvin, maybe some other time, but right now we have got to get going."

She was reluctantly taking her mouth off Melvin when Jenny came into the room and saw it. "God damn it Mrs. Clayton, he's mine. Leave him the fuck alone."

She had had enough of Jenny's attitude and she barked back, "Don't give me any of your shit little girl. You are the one who told your dad, not once, but three times that he should give Melvin a shot a my ass."

"She's got you there, Jenny. Come on and get dressed, we need to get home to your mother."

"There isn't any hurry pops. As long as I'm with you she isn't going to suspect you of fooling around."

"True baby girl, but we still need to get home."

As Melvin dressed he looked at her and she saw the hunger in his eyes and she smiled at him and silently mouthed the words, "You'll get your chance."

When Dave, Jenny and Melvin were gone she tried to get Brian up one more time, but he was just plain worn out. The two of them snuggled up and fell into a deep, relaxing sleep.

~~***~~

When she woke up in the morning she tried again, but half hard was the best he could get and that wasn't going to help her at all. She fixed breakfast for the two of them and then told him he needed to leave because Sunday was when her mother and sister came to visit.

"Tonight then? After they are gone?"

"No Brian. I need a night of rest."

"Tomorrow then?"

"Call me, we'll see."

Chapter 5

She awoke Monday morning and she felt like she was going through withdrawal. Sunday had been the first day in weeks that she hadn't had a cock. The day had been a nervous and irritable one for her and her mother had asked her if she was feeling well. After her mother and sister had gone she had spent the rest of the day cleaning house while feeling fidgety and then that night she hadn't slept for beans.

She was eager to get to work and into Dave's office. It didn't matter what he wanted, pussy, ass or mouth as long as she got some cock. Dave didn't disappoint her. By nine-fifteen she had been fucked and the nervousness and irritability were gone and she was looking forward toward their nooner. She got the call at eleven-thirty and her pussy was already wet and dripping as she headed for Dave's office. As soon as she was in the office she went to remove her panties and Dave told her not too. He told her they were going out to lunch and that he had a surprise for her. She asked what kind of a surprise and got the predictable.

"It wouldn't be a surprise if I told now wouldn't it."

The divider was down between the front and back of the limo and on the way to the restaurant her eyes met Melvin's in the rear view mirror. She smiled and winked at him and he quickly looked away. She was curious about what it would be like to have sex with a black man and she was going to find some way to give Melvin what he wanted. Then she had a random thought; maybe she shouldn't give Melvin what he wanted. What if there was truth to the saying that if you go black you never go back. She just wanted an experience, not a commitment.

Lunch was at the Hilton and was enjoyable and when it was over Dave led her to the elevators and they took one up to the seventh floor and went into room 721.

"What's my surprise?"

"It will be here shortly, but while we wait I'd like a little head."

She giggled as she went to her knees in front of him and reached for his zipper. "Is that all you think of?"

"It is when you are around."

She was just starting to lick Dave's balls when there was a knock on the door and Dave said, "Your surprise is here." He pulled his cock from her sucking mouth and went to answer the door. He opened the door and two men that she recognized as clients of her firm came in.

"Sarah, you know Sam and Don. They just renewed their contracts with us and I thought it would be a nice gesture on my part to show them how much we appreciate their business. They have both, at one time or another, commented on how beautiful and sexy you look and so I thought what better way to say thank you than to give them a taste of you."

She was still kneeling on the floor next to the bed and as she looked at the three men she knew she should get up and leave the room. It was getting just too complicated. First Brian, and then Brian and Dave and almost Melvin and now this – two more – and if she did it where would it end? Would it end? Would she continue to take on more and more cock until finally one day it would be impossible to hide it from Tim?

"Come on Sarah, no need to be shy. You know you want this. I've known since that first time with Brian that you have been curious about what three men at the same time would be like. Here's your chance to find out."

Dave was right, she had wondered what three would be like and she did have one more week before Tim came home. What better time to satisfy all of her curiosities and get them all out of the way so she could go back to being Tim's and only Tim's. Yes, why not. She stood up and began to unbutton her blouse. She stripped her clothes off and then she went to her knees and crawled over to Dave and reached out a hand and rubbed the bulge in his pants. She unbuckled his belt and then she hooked her fingers in his waistbands and pulled his trousers and briefs down at the same time. Released form confinement his stiff cock bobbed up and down in front of her face. She looked up into his face, smiled and then she leaned forward and took his cock into her mouth. She sucked it for several seconds and then took her mouth off Dave and looked back over her shoulder at Sam and Don who were standing there watching, but still dressed.

"Well? Are you going to play with us or not?"

Both men hurriedly started to undress and she turned her attention back to Dave's cock. She kissed the tip and then reached for his balls. As she caressed them she slowly worked her tongue and lips on his cock. She felt some one move in behind her and fingers start rubbing on her wet pussy. The fingers slowly parted her pussy lips and pressed into her. She moaned and pushed back at the man behind her. Suddenly the fingers were removed and she felt a hard cock pushing at her. Once again she moaned and shoved back and the cock slid right into her soaking wet pussy. She trembled with excitement as she thought about the third cock still to come.

"Let's take this to the bed," Dave said and as she got to her feet she saw that it had been Don who had been in her pussy. She looked over at Sam and saw that he had the skinniest cock of the three men and she decided that he would be the first one in her ass.

As they got on the bed she told Dave to stand at the head of the bed and lean against the wall. She told Don to lie down on his back and when he did she moved over him and squatted down on his hard cock taking it into her as far as it would go. She looked over at Sam and said:

"You know where I want you Sam, but go slow okay?"

She leaned forward until she was lying on Don's chest, which elevated her ass for Sam. He moved in behind her and worked a finger into her ass and started working at loosening her up. Then the finger came out and a thumb slid into and started probing and a minute or so later she felt the head of a still cock poke at her butt hole. Sam popped past her sphincter and then slowly worked his cock deep into her ass. She moaned and pushed herself down on Don's cock. She had never felt so full and she moaned as Don started fucking up into her as Sam went deeper into her ass.

She propped herself up on her hands and leaned forward and took Dave's cock back into her mouth. Don pushed up into her, which pushed her back at Sam. Sam thrust into her and that drove her down on Don. The two men worked at establishing a rhythm and when they managed to achieve it she had a massive orgasm. Dave grabbed her head and started to fuck her mouth and she gave herself over to the three men.

It was four hours later when the three men called it quits and left her lying on the bed like a wet dishrag. As they dressed Dave asked:

"How about it Sarah, want to do this again sometime?"

She smiled weakly and gave a little wave with her hand and Dave laughed and said to Don and Sam, "I think that was a yes."

~~***~~

When she got home she found Brian parked in her driveway. He got out of his car and walked up to her as she was unlocking the front door.

"Where have you been?"

"I had to work late."

"Well don't you think that you could at least…"

"Whoa up there, Brian. You have no claim on me and you have no rights other than those I choose to give you. You are not my husband and where I go, what I do and what time I come home is none of your damned business. When you left yesterday and asked about today I told you to call me and we'd see. Have you talked with me today?"

"No, but…"

"But nothing. I didn't tell you that you could come over tonight so why are you here?"

Just then the phone started ringing and she rushed into the house and grabbed the cordless phone to answer it. It was Tim. As she talked to him she walked over to the couch, slipped her panties off and sat down on the edge of the couch. She spread her legs wide and used the hand not holding the phone to point at her naked pussy. Brian smiled and dropped his trousers exposing his already hard cock. He got down on his knees in front of her and was lining himself up when she nodded her head no and pointed to her mouth. He understood; she wanted her pussy eaten.

He lowered his head and as soon as his tongue slipped between her pussy lips he knew he had been sand bagged. He went to pull back, but by then she had a handful of his hair and she held him against her cunt and pushed it up at his face. He went to grab her arm and as he did he she said, "Just a minute baby, I have to blow my nose."

She covered the mouth piece of the phone with her hand and leaned down and whispered, "Do it or get the hell out."

She let go of his hair and went back to talking to her husband:

"No baby, I was just getting home when you called."

"Just a very busy day. I spent all afternoon in contract negotiations with Dave and two clients."

"What's that?"

"Yes, I guess you could say it was successful. I'm pretty sure that by the time we concluded all parties were satisfied."

"Yes, I guess you could say that I seem to have what it takes. Dave is thinking of letting me do more of it."

"Yes, I think I'm going to try it, at least for a while. I get a charge out of getting them to see things my way and do what I want them to do."

"No baby, I just got home and I haven't eaten yet, but eating is something that is very high on my list of priorities right now." As she said that she threw a very pointed look at Brian and he got the message. He buried his face deep in her fur and started lapping.

"No, I'm thinking of eating a hot dog when I hang up, maybe even a couple. Enough about my day baby. How did yours go?"

"Are you alone?"

"You know exactly what I mean hubby dear. Is some sweet, young San Diego slut sucking your cock right now while you are talking to me?"

"What do you mean, 'don't be silly.'? I know how much you like sex and men are such weak willed creatures."

"No dear, women have more will power than men. I will admit that being without you has me horny enough to climb walls, but I can sit here on the couch and cope. You, on the other hand, get to sit around in the hotel cocktail lounge and since you are a sexy looking guy I know that you are getting a lot of come ons from the lonely ladies. All I have here are pictures on the wall to look at me."

"No baby, I'm sitting on the couch with my panties off, my legs spread wide as I finger myself while imagining you eating my pussy. I can feel your tongue sliding into me. I can just feel your lips sucking on my clit. Your cock is throbbing and I know you are aching to slide it into me, but I put a hand on your head to hold you in place because I'm so close to cumming. You can feel the nearness of my explosion and you work harder at getting me off."

Brian was doing just what she was telling Tim she was imagining and then suddenly she cried out, "Oh yes, yes, yeS, yES, YES!" as Brian sucked her to an orgasm.

"What?" she mumbled into the phone.

"Oh that. I just fingered myself to an orgasm. Hurry up and get home baby, I need a cock in me bad."

Brian heard that and he lined his cock up with her pussy and pushed it in. She clenched her teeth together to keep from moaning or crying out and said:

"Take lots of vitamins baby because I don't plan on letting you out of bed for a week after you get home. You will have to call in sick because you won't have enough strength to crawl out of bed."

"To hell with Brian and your work load. Just tell him that your wife has a very bad case of the hornies and she needs you to see that she gets well."

"What do you mean he wouldn't understand? Hell, bring him home with you and let him see what a hot horny bitch I can be when I've gone without."

"I don't know baby, would you want me to? He is kind of cute and it would ease the pressure on you."

"Okay, okay, but you brought it up, I didn't. The bathroom is calling me baby so I need to go."

"I love you too baby, good night. I'll talk to you tomorrow."

She pushed the off button on the phone and dropped it on the couch next to her and wrapped her arms around Brian.

"Fuck me you bastard, fuck me hard and make me cum."

Later in bed, after their third coupling of the evening Brian asked her about her conversation with Tim, especially the part about bringing Brian home with him.

"He said that if he did that you would probably want a piece of me for yourself."

"Would he do that? I mean would he let me if I did come home with him?"

"Of course not. He got pissed when I said I thought you were cute and that it might take some of the pressure off of him."

She felt his cock twitch against her leg and she got on her knees and put her head down on the pillow. "My ass this time lover, do my ass this time."

~~***~~

The rest of the week went by quickly. Brian spent the night Monday and Tuesday and when their morning session was over on Wednesday morning she told him that it was the last time for them.

"Tim will be home Friday and I think I should let my pussy tighten up a bit for him."

"How about our Tuesdays?"

"Maybe, but not for a while. I need to concentrate on my husband for a while. Call me in a couple of weeks."

The week at work was also pretty much what she expected. Tuesday was Dave and the president of Apex Industries; Wednesday was Dave and two guys from Denex Corporation. After she was done with them she told Dave the same thing she had told Brian – no more strange cock, she had to be ready for Tim.

"And Dave? No more at the office for a couple of weeks."

"Not even blowjobs?"

She thought for a minute and then said, "Okay, we can do blow jobs, but Tim is the only one getting any pussy for a while."

~~***~~

When Tim walked in the front door at five thirty-seven on Friday, she met him at the door wearing thigh high nylons and 'Come Fuck Me' pumps with five-inch heels. She handed him a martini:

"Sip on this sailor while I unwrap the present you brought me."

She sank to her knees in front of him and worked his trousers and briefs off of him. His cock was bouncing in front of her face and as she looked at it she wondered why she was doing what she was doing with Dave and Brian when she had such a great cock at home. Maybe Dave had been right when he said that there was a slut in her that had just been waiting to be set free. She looked up at Tim and smiled.

"I hope you did what I suggested baby and took lots and lots of vitamins," and then she opened her mouth and took him in.

For the next two weeks she didn't leave Tim alone. He got a quickie every morning before going to work and there were nights when dinner sat uneaten on the stove. The weekends were almost non-stop sex. The third Monday Tim was home, he came home from work and found her naked and waiting for him. He dropped his briefcase on the floor and started to unbutton his shirt as he said, "I've got to get Brian to send me out of town again just so I can get some rest."

"Oh poor baby, getting too much loving? Tell you what. You do a good job on me tonight and I'll give you tomorrow off."

"What do you consider a good job?"

"Make love to me until I pass out."

"You know I can't do that. You always make me pass out."

"That'll work," and she took his hand and led him to the bedroom.

~~***~~

Tuesday morning as she finished giving Dave his morning blowjob he said, "I need a favor from you."

"What?"

"I'm supposed to have lunch with Howie Martin today. He has a signed contract that I have to pick up, but something else has come up and I can't make it. I need you to sub for me."

"That's all? Just have lunch and pick up a signed contract?"

"That's all."

"You sure you haven't pimped me to him?"

"No Sarah, straight deal. Have lunch with him, get the contract and get it back here."

"What time?"

"The Hilton at eleven. Melvin will run you over there, wait for you and then bring you back."

At ten-thirty she was sitting in the back of the limo watching Melvin watch her in the rear view mirror. She thought back to the night she'd had his cock in her mouth and she wondered if the chance would ever come again. She looked at her watch as if she was wondering if there was time to have him park somewhere and get in the back with her, but of course there wasn't. She wondered what he was thinking. Was he wondering how his cock would feel in her butt? Or was he thinking about the night he had been in her mouth for those few seconds. "No, damn it! Stop thinking like that," she told herself. Aside from Dave's daily blowjob you have been good. Just need to work on eliminating sucking Dave's cock and it can be just you and Tim again.

The lunch with Howie Martin was pleasant and when it was over he apologized for not having the contract with him.

"I was expecting Dave and he and I usually have a drink or two in my room and tell each other war stories. I'll have to run up and get it. Just have a seat in the lobby and I'll be right back down."

"That isn't necessary, I'll just go up with you. It will save you some time."

"You sure you don't mind?"

"Positive."

Once inside the room Howie went to his briefcase and took out some papers and he turned to her just in time to see her skirt hit the floor.

~~***~~

It was four o'clock when she got back to the office and dropped the signed contracts on Dave's desk. He looked up at her and smiled.

"I just got off the phone with Howie. He tells me he loves the messenger service I use. Does this mean I can look forward to more than just blowjobs now?"

She lifted her skirt up to her waist and bent forward over Dave's desk, leaned on it and waited. Dave moved up behind her and she moaned, "My ass Dave, do my ass."

For the rest of the week it was a blowjob for Dave first thing every morning and at least one session on the leather couch at lunch time or in the afternoon at quitting time. Friday, Brian called her and asked if she were ready to see him again on Tuesdays and she told him that she didn't think that it would be a good idea.

"I think it is a great idea. In fact, I'll make you a deal. You see me every Tuesday for a long lunch and I promise I won't send Tim out of town any more."

She thought about that for a moment or two. Now that she was back to screwing Dave she had eased up on Tim a little and she would rather have him home than gone.

"You promise, no more trips?"

"I promise."

"Okay Brian, we have a deal."

Chapter 6

The next three months went quickly by. She was giving Tim all the sex he could handle, seeing to Dave's needs (and the needs of several of his better customers) and seeing Brian every Tuesday. The only fly in the ointment, at least from her standpoint, was that every time she tried to get something going with Melvin something always got in the way. Four times she was almost sure she had him alone, but each time either Dave or Jenny did something to prevent her from trying on Melvin.

It all came crashing down on a Monday in October. She got a call from Brian:

"We have to cancel tomorrow sweetie, and probably all the rest of our Tuesdays."

"Why? What is going on?"

"Tim came to see me this morning and asked for some time off. I asked why and he said he had some personal problems that needed to be looked into. I pushed him and he blurted out that he thinks you are cheating on him and he wants the time off to follow you and see what you are up to. I had to give him the time off sweetie, so watch your back. I'm going to miss you babe."

As she hung up her heart was beating fast. The one thing she never wanted to happen was happening. What had she done to make Tim suspect her? She thought back, but couldn't think of anything she might have let slip. She went into Dave's office and told him about Brian's phone call.

"It is over Dave. No more playing. Tim will be watching me like a hawk now and I don't dare do anything that might give what we've been doing away."

"Don't worry sweetie. What goes on in this building he has no way of seeing."

"No Dave, no more. I don't want to take the chance of making the least little slip. I can't lose Tim, I'd die if he left me."

"Go on back to your office sweetie and let me think on this."

That night at home she tried to see if Tim was any different around her, but she saw no signs that he was suspicious. Could Brian have been wrong? He wasn't, and she got the proof the next day.

Dave called her into his office ten minutes after she got to work. "Tim is parked just down the block in a rental car and he's watching the building. I guess he thinks you leave here during the day to meet your lover or lovers."

"How do you know that?"

"I hired a private investigator to watch him and keep me informed as to his movements."

He took out his cock and waved it at her.

"I'm not doing that any more Dave."

"Yes you will, Sarah. You will because I want it and you want it. I agree with you that now Tim is suspicious it isn't worth the risk any more, but I want one last day. You are going to be mine all day Sarah and then I'll never touch you again unless you come and ask me. Now please suck my cock while I tell you what we are going to do."

She had sucked Dave's cock, deep throating him the way he liked, and after she had swallowed his cum she had sucked him hard again and then moved to the leather couch and spread herself wide for him. After taking a load in her pussy she had again sucked him hard and then she had leaned over the back of the couch and let Dave take her ass.

"How does it feel to know that your husband is right outside just down the block while I fuck you. Does it excite you?"

"Yes," she had panted as Dave drove his cock up her butt.

"Does it turn you on to cheat on him while knowing that he is trying to catch you with another man's dick in you?"

"Yes, oh God, oh God yes, yes, yes. Fuck me lover, fuck me hard and make me cum."

Dave pulled her off the couch and led her over to the large window. She leaned down and put her hands on the windowsill and spread her legs and moaned when Dave slid back into her ass.

"See that black Honda Accord parked down there? That's your hubby Sarah. He's trying to catch your cheating ass. He wants to catch you having a good time. Are you having a good time Sarah?'

"Oh God yes Dave. I love you in my ass, fuck me lover, fuck me."

"Look down at him Sarah. He can't see you through this tinted glass, but you can see him. Does it excite you to watch him while I fuck you Sarah?"

She moaned and shoved her ass back at him.

"Can you see his eyes Sarah, can you look into them while I fuck you?"

She moaned again, "Make me cum damn you, make me cum."

"Are you my slut Sarah?"

"Yes damn you, yes."

"Say it Sarah, say it."

"I'm your slut Dave, I'm a cheating whore and I'm your slut. Now make me cum damned you, make me cum."

She lay on the leather couch, legs splayed wide and with a teardrop shaped blob of cum barely hanging from her pussy lips. Dave looked down at her as he tucked his cock back into his pants.

"I hope your desk is clear and that you have nothing pressing. Since today is my last day I intend to make the most of it. Next on the list is to have some fun with your husband."

She sat up alarmed and he laughed, "Not to worry my sweet slut, he will never know, but you and I will. What we are going to do is go have lunch with Jason Boggs."

~~***~~

"Where is he?" Dave asked Melvin as the limo cruised along the highway.

"Three car lengths back."

She was naked on the rear seat (except for heels) and Dave was sliding his cock into her hot ass.

"He's only sixty or seventy feet away Sarah. How does it feel to be fucked so close to your husband?"

She moaned and gasped, "It feels so good baby, your cock feels so good."

"You like my cock in your ass while your hubby is so near?"

"I love your cock in my ass. Fuck me lover, fuck me."

"Get up on your knees and look out the back window."

She did what she was told and then he slid his cock back into her butt and started slowly stroking back and forth.

"See him back there? See him trying to catch you cheating on him? Watch his face Sarah, watch his face while I fuck your tight cheating ass. Think he suspects what you might be doing Sarah? Think he is back there saying to himself, 'I wonder if Sarah is getting fucked on the back seat of that car?'

"Fuck him and what he is thinking Dave, just fuck me, make me cum" and she shoved her ass back to meet Dave's thrusts.

"Should I open a window Sarah and tell Melvin to slow down? Maybe your hubby will speed up and pass us so he can look in the window. Would you like that Sarah? Would you like to be looking into each other's eyes when I cum in your ass?"

She shoved back harder, "Fuck me you bastard, pound my ass, make me cum."

"Where is he, Melvin?"

"Two cars back."

"Hear that Sarah? He's closing in. He's getting closer to his cheating wife. Aren't you glad for tinted windows Sarah? You can see him back there, but he can't see you. He thinks someone besides him is putting a cock in you and we know it's true, don't we?"

"Please Dave, make me cum. I'm so close lover, make me cum, get me off Dave, get me off."

"Not yet my sweet slut, not just yet. Slow down a little Melvin, maybe the car behind us will get impatient and pull out and pass us. That will leave the slut's husband right behind us"

The limo slowed and moments later she saw the car behind them pull out to pass and the black Accord moved up. She could see Tim and she could almost see his eyes.

"See him Sarah? See how close he is? Do you think he knows how close he is to his wife while she lets another man fuck her? Does it excite you Sarah to be looking into his face while I'm cumming in you?"

She was looking into Tim's face when she felt Dave's cum splash inside her and she responded with a screaming orgasm of her own.

"Get dressed Sarah, we're almost to the restaurant."

~~***~~

She was reviewing the contract language with Jason when Dave's cell phone rang. He took the call and when he disconnected he said:

"That was the private detective. He says your husband is sitting in the coffee shop where he can watch us. Just act natural and don't look that way."

He put the phone away and said, "How about it Jason, ready to sign on the dotted line?"

"I don't know. I was supposed to get an afternoon with Sarah, but you tell me her husband is following her. She was my incentive to sign with you and it looks like it isn't going to happen."

"Do you like kinky Jason?"

"Depends on what you mean by kinky?"

"How would you like to enjoy Sarah while her hubby is only sixty or seventy feet away and completely unaware that you are doing her?"

"You serious?"

"Absolutely."

"When?"

"As soon as we finish lunch and you hand Sarah a signed contract."

"You have a pen?"

"Yes indeed I do. Ready to be a slut again Sarah?"

"Yes Dave."

"Tell Jason what you are Sarah."

She looked at Jason, "I'm Dave's slut. I am a cheating whore of a wife and I'm Dave's slut."

They were cruising down the highway and Sarah was sitting between Dave and Jason. Their flies were open and their cocks were sticking up. She had a cock in each hand and was slowly stroking them both when Dave asked:

"Where is he, Melvin?"

"Three cars back."

"Okay Sarah, I'm going to open the window on the driver's side. When hubby pulls up alongside of us I want you to be jacking us off just a little harder than you are now. I want you looking over at Jason like you are talking to him. I don't want you looking out the window and letting your hubby know we know he is there. Don't let him see your arm movements, but try to get one of us off just as he goes by and looks in the window. Think you can do that?"

"I don't know Dave. I don't think I can get either one of you off unless I go faster than you want me too."

"Just try Sarah, do your best. Slow down Melvin. Force the ones behind us to pass."

Melvin slowed down and after a minute the two cars between them and Sarah's husband pulled out and passed them. Tim pulled up behind them and Melvin slowed down a little more and Tim had to pull out and pass them he would call attention to himself and seconds later Melvin said:

"Here he comes."

She felt Dave's fingers push into her pussy and she moaned just as her husband drove by and looked in the window. Dave laughed:

"That's the closest you'll ever come to catching her you stupid doofus."

She let go of Dave's cock and looked at him, "What did you just call him?"

"A doofus. He's a stupid doofus."

"He is also my husband you fucking asshole. Play with your own dick from now on."

She turned her full attention to Jason. "Ready for some hot mouth honey?"

"Oh God, yes."

"You got it honey," and she lowered her head and swallowed his cock. Dave still had his fingers in her pussy and she reached down, grabbed his wrist and pulled his hand away from her.

"Sarah, don't be that way."

"Fuck you Dave. He is my husband and he doesn't deserve what I'm doing to him. I'll be god damned if I'll let you call him names just because he is unlucky enough to have a whore for a wife."

"I'm sorry Sarah, my comment was uncalled for. Please forgive me?"

Sarah ignored him and concentrated on pleasing Jason, but she didn't object when Dave slid his fingers back into her cunt. She was already hot and Dave's fingers just made her hotter.

"Where is he now, Melvin?"

"One car in front of us."

Dave put the window up. "Pass him. We don't want to lose him so it's best that he be behind us."

She was on her knees on the seat with her head in Jason's lap and Dave was just moving in behind her when they passed Tim. Dave drove his cock into her pussy and got an "Uumppf" from her and he said:

"He is less than ten feet away from your cheating ass. Does it turn you on to know that?"

She answered him by shoving her ass back at him and Dave laughed and said:

"You just think that this is your last day. You are too much of a slut to quit Sarah. I'll be fucking you until I'm too old to get it up any more."

He was wrong, but she wasn't going to argue about it just then. She had a cock in both ends of her and she was close to getting off. "Will you just shut up and fuck me?"

"Where is he Melvin?"

"Two cars back."

"Sixty feet from your hubby and you are slamming your ass back at me and telling me to fuck you. You are such a slut Sarah. I can't believe how turned on you are knowing how close he is and that he is trying to catch you at doing what you are doing."

She took her mouth off Jason and turned to him, "Will you please just shut the fuck up and fuck me. Make me cum damn it, get me off."

She lowered her head back down and took Jason's cock back in her mouth and thirty seconds later he bathed the back of her throat with his offering. She kept on sucking him until he started to stiffen again. She took her mouth off him and started jacking him off while she looked back over her shoulder at Dave and said:

"Make me cum you bastard; stop that slow shit and fuck me hard. I need to cum damn it, fuck me hard and make me cum."

Dave rammed her hard and fast and she felt her orgasm rushing at her and she raised her head and looked out the rear window and at her husband as her body shook with her climax. Dave laughed, "God what a slut you are Sarah" and then he came in her. He and Jason switched places and twenty-six miles later Jason filled her box with his seed. When Jason pulled out of her Dave told Melvin to find a gas station. Melvin filled the tank and then got back in the car.

"Where is he now, Melvin?"

"Across the street in the Safeway parking lot."

"Can he see you from where he is parked?"

"No, just the rear half of the car."

"Climb over the partition into the back."

"Sir?"

"Get back here Melvin, it's your turn."

"Yes sir!"

Once Melvin was in the back Dave climbed up front, started the limo and pulled away from the pumps. They weren't even off the gas station's lot before Melvin had his cock in her mouth. She sucked him for a minute and then let his cock slip from her lips:

"You're already hard so I need my mouth to get Jason ready. Take my ass baby, Jenny says you have always wanted my ass."

Jason's cock was already in her mouth when Melvin started to ease his cock into her back passage. She squealed around Jason's pole as Melvin pushed deeper and deeper into her and then she lost it. The wickedness of taking a black man in her ass and sucking off a man she had never met before lunch time that day while her husband was in sight was so erotically stimulating that she became a mindless piece of meat for the two men who had their cocks in her. Melvin came in her ass and then switched places with Jason (after wiping his cock off on her panties) and when Jason came they switched again.

When the limo pulled into the parking lot at work she was astride Jason who was in her pussy and bent forward looking out the rear window at the black Accord while Melvin's black cock was buried in her ass.

"Come on guys, you will have to finish in my office. If we all just sit here in a parked car her hubby could get wise."

Melvin and Dave quickly changed places and then Melvin got out of the car and opened the door for them. She unsteadily stepped out of the car and hoped that Tim was far enough away that he couldn't see the cum running down her leg.

She was on her back on Dave's desk with her legs up on Jason's shoulders, her nails biting into his back, while he plunged his cock into her pussy. Melvin had Jenny on the leather couch and was fucking her in her ass for the first time and she was squealing like a pig. Jenny had been at her desk when she Dave, Jason and Melvin had gone into her father's office. She had waited several moments before curiosity over why her boyfriend had breezed right on by without a word got to her. She had opened the office door and looked in just in time to see Melvin's cock slide into Sarah's ass while she was bent forward over Dave's desk.

"God damn you Melvin, what the hell are you doing?"

"Getting some of what you won't give me."

"Well you better stop right now if you ever expect to get any more pussy from me."

"See you!"

"What? What did you say?"

"See you around. I ain't wasting no more time on any woman who won't give me what I need."

"You don't mean that!"

"Oh, yes I do."

Tears formed in her eyes and Jenny was all set to turn and leave the room when Sarah cried out:

"Oh God, oh God, oh yes, like that, just like that, harder lover, fuck me harder."

Jenny had gotten so mad at Sarah calling Melvin "lover" that she had gone over and pulled Melvin away from Sarah and pulled him over to the couch. She pulled off her panties, got on her knees and snarled:

"You want my ass? Then take it damn you, take it" and Melvin did.

Jenny's dad was standing over at the window looking out:

"He's still there Sarah, still sitting there and watching the building. I guess he is going to follow you until you get home."

Sarah wasn't listening and right then she didn't care beans about Tim. When Jenny had pulled Melvin away from her she had been near her orgasm and she had cried out in protest. Jason had quickly moved to her and pushed her up on the desk and had mounted her. Jason had her on the ragged edge of another orgasm when Dave had made his comment about Tim.

"Fuck Tim," she had thought, "If he doesn't trust me, fuck him."

It was four-thirty before the party was over. Jenny had been possessive as hell where Melvin was concerned so Sarah had to settle for just Jason and Dave and by four-thirty neither man could answer the call again. She had gotten dressed and had gone to the ladies room to clean up before going home. As she got ready to leave the office she said to Dave:

"It has been fun lover and I'll always remember it."

"You won't stop Sarah, you are too much of a slut and we both know it. I'll give you a week and you'll be back in here licking my cock."

"No way Dave. I'm not taking any more chances on losing Tim."

~~***~~

She was home fixing dinner when Tim walked in. She greeted him with a kiss (she had brushed her teeth and gargled) and had asked him how his day had gone.

"Just another day at the salt mine. What's for dinner?"

"Vegetable linguine."

"You hate that."

"Yes, but you love it and since I'm not eating tonight I thought I would make it for you."

"Why aren't you eating?"

"I don't feel so good."

"What's wrong?"

"It was probably something I ate today. Your fault by the way.'

"My fault? How is it my fault?"

"I was able to take a long lunch today so I called you to see if you would have lunch with me, but no one could find you so I ended up going to lunch with Dave and having lunch with a customer. Where were you?"

"Probably out in the warehouse."

"Anyway, I had a large Greek salad and I'm thinking the salad might have had some bad olives or mushrooms. My stomach has been queasy all afternoon. I'm going to go upstairs and lie down. Don't worry about the dishes, I'll get them tomorrow."

"Just my luck. I was planning on getting frisky with you tonight."

"Sorry honey, but I don't think my tummy could take the bouncing. I'll give you head as long as you don't mind if I don't swallow. God knows what that would do if it got mixed in the mess that's in my stomach now."

"No sweetie, it won't kill me to go a day or two without."

Good, she thought, two days should give my pussy time to tighten up.

Whether two days would have been enough or not she never found out because on day two her period started. When Tim got home that night she offered to give him as much head as he would like and then she casually dropped the comment:

"Or we could try anal sex."

"Damn it Sarah, why do you keep after me about that? You know that I think that is disgusting and perverted."

"I keep trying Tim because I want to see what it is like. I may not even like it, but I'll never know if I don't try it. It would be perfect for times like this when I'm on the rag and it is automatic birth control. I wouldn't even have to put in my diaphragm."

"Well, it isn't going to happen Sarah so give it up."

"Yes dear."

~~***~~

The rest of the week, knowing what Tim was up to, she kept an eye on her rear view mirror and watched him follow her to work. She watched from Dave's office window as he parked down the street and watched the office and then she watched him follow her home. By Friday, she was so pissed at Tim she was sorry that she had cut off Dave. It was irrational of her and she knew it because after all she had been cheating, but she was still pissed at him that he could even think that of her. Didn't he know how much she loved him? Following her to see if she was cheating? The very idea! It would serve Tim right if she did go into Dave's office and spread herself out on the leather couch for him.

She had a lot of time to think on her drives to work and then home and she tried to think of what she had done to make Tim suspicious. She knew she hadn't said anything to give herself away. She came straight home from work every night. She didn't have a 'night out with the girls'. She had gone over their bedroom with a fine toothcomb after the two weeks Brian had slept with her so she knew he found nothing there. Could he have seen her go into the hotel on the Tuesday's she met Brian? No, not likely. They had stopped that before Brian went on his trip. The only thing she could think of was her pussy. Maybe it had started feeling different to him. Loose – could that be it? She had started feeling loose to him? She hadn't even thought about that, but with all the sex she had been having with Dave and his customers she probably wasn't as tight as Tim had been used too. Well time would take care of that and she wouldn't have that problem anymore because Tim was the only one who would ever fuck her from then on.

~~***~~

That was a lie of course. Dave had almost nailed it when he said she would be back in his office and on her knees licking his dick within a week. Actually it was three weeks and even then she told him that her pussy was off limits.

"It is Tim's pussy and only Tim's pussy. I'll give you blowjobs and since Tim won't give me anal sex you can have my butt too, but that is all. You and only you, no customers, not even one. Maybe Melvin if he can sneak past Jenny, but that's all, agreed?"

"Agreed."

Dave of course told Brian that he was back to doing her and Brian called wanting to get back in the game. She hated to do it, but she shut him down.

"I can do Dave because he is here inside the building and we have all the privacy and security we need. With you I could never be sure that Tim wouldn't follow me again or hire a private detective to do it. I'm a hundred percent safe doing it in Dave's office, but anywhere else would be a question mark."

"So I'll just come to my good old frat brother's office and we can do it there."

"No Brian, no! And I mean it. I'm not taking any more chances and when I hang up I'm telling Dave that if he lets you come over I'll cut him off cold. It was fun, I loved it, but it is over!"

Well, that was true, but only up to a point. At every one of Tim's company Christmas parties over the next fifteen years, Brian managed to get her into an office and screw her. On those nights it didn't much matter because Tim go so blitzed he wouldn't have known loose from tight even if she would have given him sloppy seconds, which of course she never did.

Epilogue

It was their twenty-fifth wedding anniversary and they were lounging by the pool at a resort hotel. She was working the New York Times crossword puzzle and he was lying on a blanket looking at her.

"Sarah, can I ask you something?"

"Of course you can love," as she tried to come up with a word for five down.

"Have you ever been unfaithful to me?"

Without looking up from her puzzle she said, "Yes dear."

"You have?"

"That's what I just said. What's a nine letter word for fatigue starting with T?"

"Tiredness. I'm not kidding Sarah."

"Neither am I my love."

"When?"

She looked up from her puzzle and stared into space as she thought back. "Let's see now. It would have been twenty, no – nineteen years ago."

"You aren't kidding me, are you?"

"No Tim, you asked, I answered."

"Who was it?"

"My boss Dave."

"For how long?"

"Five days."

"Why?"

"Because you pissed me off so bad that I let Dave have me."

"I pissed you off that bad? What the hell did I do?"

"You somehow got it in your head that I was cheating on you so you rented a car and started following me. Did you honestly think you could park down the block and watch the building and not be noticed? You thought that none of my co-workers who had seen you at countless company picnics and Christmas parties would recognize you? I hadn't been at my desk ten minutes before a dozen people wanted to know why you were parked down the street watching the building.

"It didn't take an Einstein to figure it out. I spent the entire day with people looking at me and thinking I was a slut who had been caught onto by her husband. I kept getting up and going to the window and looking out and you would always still be there. By that afternoon I was so pissed at your lack of trust that I decided if you were going to give me the name I would play the game. Dave had been coming onto me since the day I hired in so I went into his office and told him I couldn't fight it anymore, I just had to have him."

"Why only five days?"

"You only followed me for five days. You stopped following me, I stopped screwing Dave. What's a seven letter word for oracle starting with a P?"

"Prophet."

"Why did you start following me?"

"I don't know. I just had a feeling."

"Well I'm glad you had that feeling because I never would have given in to Dave otherwise."

"You were glad you gave into him?"

"You bet. I got something that I always wanted."

"What was that?"

"Anal sex. That was the deal. He could have my ass, but that was all. Mouth and pussy were yours exclusively even if you didn't trust me. I felt I could give him my pooper since you didn't want it anyway."

"Just the five days and that was the end of it?"

"Yes dear," she lied remembering all those days bent over Dave's desk while he plowed her ass; right up to and including the day before they left for this trip.

"And that was the only time?"

"Yes baby, now be a sweetie and put some more lotion on my shoulders."

"Yes dear."

The End

Here is a preview of another story you may enjoy:

JUST PLAIN BOB

FULFILLING
Her Needs

BECOMING A SHARED WIFE, VOL. 4

HOT EROTICA

"Ain't that just like a man? I'm not gone for ten minutes and he's ready to replace me."

I sat back down and gave Pam a sheepish grin and told her that I hadn't expected her back.

"You've got to be kidding! I've just spent two weeks cooped up with relatives and two rambunctious boys and you think I'm going to pass up a chance to relax and have a good time? I've put the boys to bed and outside of checking on them occasionally I expect to stay here, let you keep my glass full and my feet on the dance floor."

Just my fucking luck, I thought, everything in place to seduce her and her kids are here. Something must have shown on my face and Pam misread it. She glanced at the woman alone at the table and said;

"Or am I going to cramp your style?"

I looked back at her and smiled, "No sweetie, I'm yours for the night."

I'm not much of a drinker so after four drinks I switched to soda water, but Pam stayed with vodka tonics. We were on the floor for almost all of the dances and while the fast ones weren't much of a bother the slow ones were killers. On the slow ones Pam moved into me and it was impossible for her not to feel my erection. She didn't say a word, but she didn't back off either and I wondered if she was being a tease or if she'd a few too many vodka tonics, either way I didn't care, she might have felt my cock poking her leg, but I had those magnificent 36C's pressed into my chest. We had just finished a fast number and I said that we needed to be calling it a night since we had an early flight to catch. The band struck up a slow number and Pam said:

"Just one more. Please?"

She moved into me and every inch of me was plastered to every inch of her and my erection was almost painful. I knew I would be masturbating as soon as I got into my room and got my pants off. Her leg stayed in contact with my cock and it was all I could do to keep from kissing her. When the song ended I walked her to the rooms and she stood on tiptoe and kissed my cheek, thanked me for a very nice evening and went into her room.

I was sitting on my bed, stroking my cock, when I heard a click and the door to the adjoining room opened and Pam came in and closed the door behind her. She saw what I was doing...

To purchase this book, look for **Fulfilling Her Needs - Becoming a Shared Wife, Vol. 4** in Amazon.com.

The narrow village road looked the same. Nothing had changed since she left a few years ago. Time had left her home village behind. There were no new houses and the old ones were just as she remembered them, each set back away from the road and surrounded by flowering bushes and fruit trees.

No one was out and about at this time of day. Most of the villagers would be tending their vegetable plots and rice fields. Anna walked to a small wooden house raised five feet above the ground on short, stout timber beams.

She took off her shoes and using the dipper, scooped water from the big urn next to the steps and washed her feet, the way all the villagers did before entering their homes.

She climbed up the six steps, crossed the small verandah to the closed door. It was not locked. None of the villagers had cause to lock their homes. Everyone knew everybody and strangers never pass their way. It was as if their village had been forgotten and it remained as it had always been. Simple wooden houses were built raised off the ground in case the heavy monsoon rains caused the small stream running by the village to overflow and flood the surroundings. There were no fences, only well-worn paths leading off to the twenty or so homes, each well-tended and boasting a variety of flowering shrubs, potted plants and fruit trees.

Anna walked into the small living room. All was quiet except for the cat that purred, opening her eyes as she sensed Anna.

"Putih!" Anna called out and the cat padded over to her, rubbing its head against Anna's bare ankles.

Anna carried her small suitcase into the back room. It had not changed. The single bed with a dresser next to the window, was neatly made. The wooden chair beside the bed was still there. On it sat the cushion embroidered with a prowling tiger. The tiger stared at her, its eyes probing her innermost secrets. The cushion was one of a set of two. She had bought the set as the tiger embodied a life-changing experience for her and Song. She had given the other cushion to Song as a potent reminder of how close they came to be a meal for the tiger. Song, his name threatened to push her into places she had no wish to revisit.

She had come home. This was the room of her childhood and adolescence, her refuge from the storms that had ripped her life apart at a tender age. Her grandparents had taken her in and raised her in this little village ever since she was five.

She looked at the photographs hanging on the wall. There were three altogether.

One showed Anna as a young child with her parents, Zul and Ainee.

The second showed Anna in school uniform clutching a trophy, flanked by her beaming grandparents.

The third showed Anna alone, with the iconic Petronas Twin Towers of Kuala Lumpur in the background.

Her life history depicted by these three photographs left big blanks that strained the curiosity of those who had come to know Anna and visited her village home.

The dream did not fade over time, not like her grandma had said it would. She used to wake up screaming, cowering in fear and her grandma would rush in and hold her, rocking her gently, murmuring words of love and assurance until her sobs subsided into hiccups and she fell asleep in Grandma's arms.

As she grew older, she learned to stifle her screams with her pillow and not wake her grandparents because they had to get up early to tend to their rice field about half a kilometer away from their village.

The first photograph triggered sketchy memories of her parents.

Her mother was a beautiful woman with big flashing eyes and red lips that often parted in a wide smile. Her father was short, like her grandfather, but had broad shoulders.

Anna remembered his strong arms whenever he lifted her into the air and she would scream in delight. She also remembered the big fights whenever mama came home late and there was no dinner on the table for papa, no dinner for Anna, who had been alone in the flat when papa unlocked the front door.

To purchase this book, look for **The Red Peony by Denise Denton.**

Also by this Author:

The Prodigal Family: The Abbotts

Watching My Shared Wife

The Waitress and the Runaway Husband

Baiting Mr. Little

Too Hot for Henry

Chuck's Fantasy

Wife Sharing and Other Adventures

The Redhead's Desires

Rescued at Riley's

Hazardous Wives

Wives Who Stray

His Every Fantasy

Open Mike Night

Pursuit for Revenge

From the Author

If you enjoyed any of my books then please share the love and promote my books in Amazon.

If you write me a review and send me an email I will send you a free book, or many.
(Just know that these emails are filtered by my publisher.)

Good news is always welcome.

One Last Thing, For Kindle Readers...

When you turn the page, Kindle will give you the opportunity to rate this book and share your thoughts on Facebook and Twitter. If you enjoyed my writings, would you please take a few seconds to let your friends know about it? Because... when they enjoy they will be grateful to you and so will I.

Thank You!

An Open Letter from Just Plain Bob

A message for those who like my stories, those who hate my stories, those who are indifferent and those who have yet to make up their minds.

I have often stated that I really don't care what others think about my stories, that I write for my own enjoyment and then I offer to share. If you like my stories fine and if you don't, also fine since I have already satisfied my target audience - me!

It is human nature to strive to get better. If you take up bowling your first games are going low scoring, but you will work and practice to get better and as your average climbs you may forget the game where you had three gutter balls and shot an eighty-six, but that game is still there in your past.

Your first time on the golf course you shot an eighty on the front nine, but did you settle for that being your game or did you work to improve? You may eventually get a three handicap, but that nine hole eighty is still there as part of your past.

When you hired in at your job did you say, "Cool, I got it made" and do nothing more than what you barely had to do or did you go to work thinking that, "Someday I'm going to be running this place." You might never climb that high, but human nature says that you are going to at least try.

It is the same with authors who write stories and post them on sites like Literotica. Their first stories might not be all that good, but comments and feedback along with a desire to get better drive them toward putting out a better product or to at least try.

I'm no different. My first stories might not have been all that great, but they are still there on the hard drive. I like cheating wife stories and five years ago I found my first adult site that catered to cheating wife stories. It was a pay site, but it had a policy of giving a free lifetime membership to anyone who submitted five stories to the site. How hard can that be I said to myself as I sat down and fired up the word processor and went to work.

I sent my five stories in and sat back to enjoy my free membership and a funny thing happened. I started getting feedback, most of it positive, and I became hooked. I started cranking out more stories. The site I was sending my stories to had seven categories:

Bisexual
Cream Pie

Groups
I Watch
Gang Bang
Racial
SM/BD

I know nothing about bisexual or SM/BD and I had no interest in Groups so all the stories I wrote I tailored for the four remaining categories:

Cream Pie
I Watch
Gang Bang
Racial.

I turned out eight stories a month, two for each category, which means that after five years I have over 120 stories in each of those categories and they are all still on the hard drive.

A year ago I received an email asking me why I never posted stories on Literotica. The answer? I didn't know about Lit. I pulled it up, liked what I saw, and started sending in stories to it. All new stories? No, not hardly, not with over 400 stories sitting on the hard drive. Maybe one new story for each fifteen or so old ones. The newer ones are better, at least I think they are and I have received some feedback that leads me to believe that others think so too, and I will continue to write new ones.

But I am still going to recycle what is on the hard drive, stories that were written specifically to fit the four categories. That means that those of you who hate cream pie stories still have eighty or so to look forward to. Ditto for those who call me a racist; you will get another seventy or so interracial stories.

Those who hate wimps will only see about fifty more of those because the stories I sent to the I Watch category were split 50/50 between what some call wimps and some call "real men." Why the 50/50 split? It came from listening to the readers. I would get feedback asking me why all the men in my stories were hard asses. "In real life men are more forgiving, especially if it is the first indiscretion." So I would write stories with forgiving husbands and boyfriends and then the next batch of feedback would say, "Why are all your husbands spineless wimps" and I'd write stories that went back the other way.

Eventually I came to realize that I was wasting my time - there was no way I could write a story that would satisfy everybody and that is when I adopted my philosophy of writing for my own enjoyment and then offering to share.

As far as the gangbang stories? Well, what can I say? Gangbangs are gangbangs and there are still eighty or so of them to go.

The bottom line is that Literotica readers are going to see more of my old stories than my new ones. If I'm still around three or four years from now it will probably go the other way, more new than old.

I feel the need to respond to some of the comments and emails I have received. By far the largest percentage comes from people who say, "You are an asshole because all women are not whores and sluts and that's all you make them out to be."

Next most common is, "You must really hate women you sick fuck."

"You must be a wimp because all the men in your stories are wimps" is up there in the top ten along with, "Why don't you give it a rest and go crawl off in a hole somewhere."

There is a lot more, but I'm only going to address those four and in reverse order.

I won't stop and go crawl in a hole because I am enjoying the hell out of what I am doing and remember what I said, I am doing this for MY OWN ENJOYMENT and then I offer to share. Some obviously like my sharing with them and so I will continue to do so. No one is holding a gun to a reader's head and telling them they must click on a Just Plain Bob story or die. It is a conscious choice on the reader's part to move that mouse and click on that story.

When a man finds out he has a cheating wife or girlfriend there are only a limited number of ways he can handle it. If he loves her he can forgive, try to forget and try to hold on and somehow make things work. He can turn his back on her, walk away and get on with his life. The third option is to take revenge.

According to a good portion of those who send me feedback the first and second options are proof that the men are wimps. If the man takes the third option he is still considered a wimp if he doesn't do some sort of physical damage to the woman and her lover. These readers believe that the only way not to be a wimp is to kill, maim and destroy everything in sight. Doing that however, will invariably get the man throw in jail and that is why it so rarely happens in real life.

In real life most revenge takes place in the man's head when he says to himself, "I should have _____ (fill in the blank) the fucking cunt!" I know this because I have been there and done that (see The Dark Trilogy). In my stories I try to mirror real life so kill, maim and destroy are going to be for the most part absent. Outside of some fisticuffs there will be very little physical violence in my stories. Most of my husbands are going to do what I did, what several of my friends and others that I know have done, forgive, or walk away. If this makes them wimps and me a wimp for writing the story that way, so be it.

Next is the "I must hate all women." Nothing could be farther from the truth. I love women. I lust after women. I even like whores and sluts. I have been married four times, engaged two other times (that did not end in marriage) and I have always had girlfriends between marriages. My philosophy is that women were put on this earth for me to enjoy and I'm not talking just sexually. I could sit at the mall (and have) for hours and just girl watch.

The engagements, girlfriends and three of the four marriages bring me to the #1 anti JPB comment on the list.

"You are an asshole because all women aren't whores and sluts."

Well dear reader, you can not prove that by me! I will say up front that I KNOW all women aren't whores and sluts, BUT the majority of the women in my life were. My mother ran around on my father for years while he was driving a truck for a living. My Aunt Margaret cheated regularly on my Uncle Bill, as did my Aunt Mildred on my Uncle Paul. My Aunt Betty fucked around on my Uncle Bob for years and finally left him for his brother, my Uncle Wendell. Uncle Wendell in turn caught her on her knees at his company Christmas party giving Season's Greetings to his boss.

My sister is three times divorced and each divorce came about when the then current husband caught her out spreading pollen. Both of the engagements I mentioned ended when I found out that I was not the one and only and a lot of the girls I dated between marriages never made it to engagement status for the same reason.

And that brings me to my three ex-wives. The first one, Helen (I believe I commented on her in the intro to The Dark Trilogy) had seven different lovers before I found out what was going on. I was living proof that love is blind. Ditto with my second wife. She had a secret life that she hid from me and when I found out about her brother, his friends and the gangbangs she was history.

My third marriage ended in divorce because of a different kind of cheating (and I can just imagine the outrage I am going to get over this) - she cheated on me with an idea. I was away from home on business, she was lonely, a couple of Jehovah's Witnesses knocked on the door and my wife, with nothing better to do invited them in. When I came home from my trip I found out that she had found God. On a scale that runs from TRUE BELIEVER on one end to ATHEIST on the other you will find me just to the right of AGNOSTIC and since I would not allow myself to be SAVED the marriage eventually died.

So yes, I write about sluts and whores because as everyone knows, you tend to write about the things you know. And I do like sluts and whores, just not the ones that lie to me and cheat on me.

So be forewarned - if you click on a Just Plain Bob story you will be getting sluts, whores and husbands who do not kill, maim and destroy. There are other things you will rarely find in a Just Plain Bob story. Even though I try to mirror real life my stories all take place in StoryLand. In StoryLand STDs and unwanted pregnancies do not exist unless the author feels like they may add something to the story. Bad things do not happen in StoryLand unless the author so wills it and no amount of "You should have…" in comments and feedback will change a story already posted.

Lastly, I will touch on a truth. None of what I have written here means shit because the same readers will still read the same stories that they profess to hate and make the same comments they have always made. Knowing this, I will deliberately post stories that will have them frothing at the mouth.

It is the least I can do for an adoring public.

Thank you!

Just Plain Bob
justplainbob@awesomeauthors.org

www.ingramcontent.com/pod-product-compliance
Lightning Source LLC
Chambersburg PA
CBHW071340130626

46556CB00004B/1955